STORM at the SUMMIT

of Mount Everest

by Ryan Jacobson and Deb Mercier

Illustrated by David Hemenway

Adventure Publications, Inc.
Cambridge, MN

DEDICATION

For Lora, I knew your obsession with Mount Everest would come in handy some day.　　　—Ryan

For Cole and Kallan, may you always help each other off the mountain.　　　—Deb

ACKNOWLEDGEMENTS

A special thanks to Dan Downing, Chris Henderson and Dana Kuznar.

Edited by Brett Ortler
Cover design by Jonathan Norberg

10 9 8 7 6 5 4 3 2 1

Copyright 2011 by Ryan Jacobson and Deb Mercier
Published by Adventure Publications, Inc.
820 Cleveland Street South
Cambridge, MN 55008
1-800-678-7006
www.adventurepublications.net

ISBN: 978-1-59193-275-8

STORM at the
SUMMIT

of Mount Everest

HOW TO USE THIS BOOK

As you read *Storm at the Summit of Mount Everest*, you will sometimes be asked to jump to a distant page. Please follow these instructions. Sometimes you will be asked to choose between two or more options. Decide which is best, and go to the corresponding page. (But be careful; some of the options will lead to disaster.) Finally, if a page offers no instructions or choices, simply turn to the next page.

Remember, *this is a story*. The characters are motivated by fame and fortune, which creates more drama and makes your decisions harder. In truth, it is a rare climber who is motivated by these things. Climbers climb for the thrill and for the challenge. Accomplishment is their reward.

This book is not intended to replace professional advice and/or training. The publisher and the authors disclaim any liability for any loss or injury that may result from the use of the information.

Please, respect all wildlife and nature. Enjoy the story, and good luck!

P.S. It may be wise to keep a bookmark handy, just in case you make a mistake and need to go back.

TABLE OF CONTENTS

PROLOGUE

Climbing Mount Everest isn't something you decide to do one day. It's something you plan for years. First of all, it isn't cheap. There's the training, equipment, permits and airplane tickets. There's time away from home, which means food and other supplies. And let's not forget the fee for being on an expedition team. Altogether, it costs more than $100,000 per person. This expedition includes both you and your sister—so that price doubles.

Secondly, climbing Mount Everest takes a lot of time: eight weeks or longer. People don't just travel to Everest, climb to the top and then go home. No, it's a series of ups and downs. Literally.

You climb a little ways. Then you climb back. You climb a little higher. Then you climb down again. Repeat. Repeat. Repeat. After all, the higher you go, the thinner the air gets. And the thinner the air gets, the harder it is to breathe. Climbers need days, and even weeks, for their bodies to adjust.

Your trip to the world's tallest mountain, located in Asia near China's southwestern border, is a dream come true. But it's so much more than that. If you and your sister reach the summit (and make it down again), you will be the youngest climbers ever to do so. And with a record like that, you'll make a ton of money. Books will be written; movies will be made. You'll be interviewed on every channel. You'll star in your own TV commercials. There's even talk of a video game based on your climb!

So far, so good. You've made it to the fourth and final camp, your last stop before the summit. Most of the hard work is already behind you. You hiked up to Base Camp, more than 17,000 feet above sea level, and you stayed there for many days to get used to the higher altitude.

Base Camp was your "home," and every moment since you arrived has been a struggle to get energized and catch your breath. Thankfully, the Sherpas are with you to help. They live near the mountain, so their bodies are better adapted to these higher altitudes.

Expedition teams hire Sherpas to carry supplies up the mountain, to set up tents and to help the paying climbers however they can. Without your team's Sherpas, you would not have made it this far.

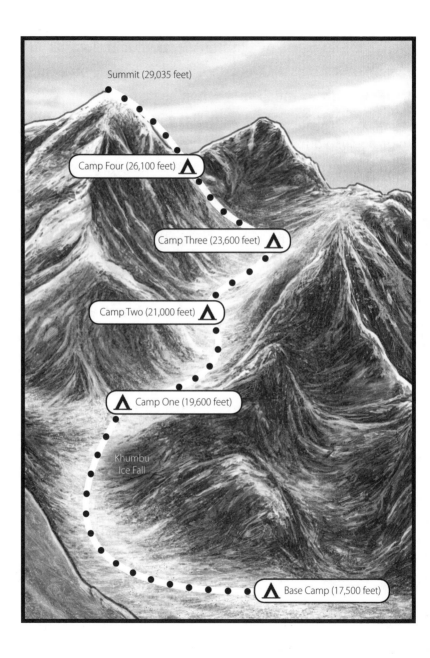

Summit (29,035 feet)

Camp Four (26,100 feet)

Camp Three (23,600 feet)

Camp Two (21,000 feet)

Camp One (19,600 feet)

Khumbu
Ice Fall

Base Camp (17,500 feet)

Your first trip farther up the mountain was to the Khumbu Ice Fall, one of the most dangerous places on Everest. Here, the ice moves and shifts at random. If a climber is in the wrong place when it does, he could get seriously hurt—or killed. There are also huge crevasses that must be crossed by walking over ladders tied together. (The Ice Fall has been your least favorite part of Mount Everest, and you've had to cross it several times.)

The next day, you climbed from Base Camp to Camp One, about 19,600 feet above sea level. You spent the night in a tent before returning to Base Camp.

That was followed by a climb and a four-night stay at Camp Two—21,000 feet high—before returning to Base Camp again.

Next you went up and slept at Camp Two, and up at Camp Three, at 23,600 feet. Then it was back to Camp Two. And back to Base Camp.

After all of that, it was finally time for the big push to the top of Mount Everest. You climbed to Camp Two and slept. Then you spent a night in Camp Three. And now you've made it to Camp Four, where you're waiting to go for the summit . . .

1

CAMP FOUR

You can't believe it: You're actually here. A tent's thin nylon walls are all that stand between you and the cold, cruel air. You're 26,100 feet above sea level, at Mount Everest's Camp Four. It took more than a year of training for your parents to let you and your twin sister, Zoey, go on this expedition. Weightlifting, aerobics, running, even yoga—you and Zoey have done it all. Ugh! The thought of yoga makes you groan.

Zoey looks up from checking her backpack for the hundredth time. "What's wrong, Zach?"

As twins, you've always been able to read each others' moods almost instantly.

"Nothing, Zo. Just yoga."

Zoey laughs. "I didn't like yoga and balance training either. Worth it, though," she adds. She grabs another pair of glove liners and stuffs them into her pack.

"I know what you mean," you tell her. "Mom and Dad have invested everything, even the house. We have a shot at being the youngest climbers ever to reach Mount Everest's summit."

Zoey grins. "Yep, if we make it, fortune and fame will be ours."

Unfortunately, the opposite is also true. Neither of you says it aloud. But you know that, if you fail, the corporate sponsors ready to pay millions will scatter to the wind. They'll whisk away like the snow outside your tent. Your family will be broke—and homeless.

You hear heavy boots crunching toward your small shelter. The front of your tent shakes, and the zipper rakes open. A rough, bearded face appears in the opening.

"Hey, Uncle Ned," you say, shivering as a blast of cold wind hits you.

Ned's face breaks into a grin. "Almost ready?"

You check your watch. It's 10:30 p.m. Your team leaves for the summit in half an hour.

"We'll be ready," you answer.

Ned laughs and melts back into the night.

He's the other reason your parents let you come to Mount Everest. Your family is a climbing family and has been for as long as you can remember. Your mom and dad even met on Mount McKinley's Karsten Ridge.

Ned, your mom's brother, runs Mountain Quest. It's a mountain climbing service that helps people reach the tallest peak in the world: mighty Mount Everest. If it weren't for Ned, you probably wouldn't be here.

Zoey pauses and looks up from her pack, her eyes wide and serious. She twists a strand of blonde hair around her finger. "You really think we're ready, Zach?"

The question surprises you. Of course you're ready. Didn't you make it all the way to Camp Four? Haven't you spent the past few weeks climbing up and down between the other camps? You've already shown this mountain who's boss. What's another 3,000 feet?

"Come on, Zoey," you say. "We've been training for, like, ever. Besides, we've got Ned and a whole team of people out there. What's the worst that can happen?"

Zoey doesn't answer; she doesn't have to. You know what she's thinking. Since the first climbers attempted to reach the summit in the early 1920s, more than 200 people have died, mostly on their way down. Conditions near the top of the mountain are so dangerous, it's called the "death zone." Many bodies remain frozen there, within view of the trail, because it would be too difficult to bring them down the mountain.

You force away a shiver and you grab your pack. It's already filled with most of what you need, but you have some extra room. There are a few more things you'd like to bring, but not all of it will fit. After you shift your gear around, you have room for four more items.

To choose four items, turn to page 64.

You reach into your bag, but you find nothing inside to help your sister. Unsure what to do, you wave Uncle Ned over to you.

He takes one look at Zoey and instantly understands the situation.

"Zoey is really struggling," you tell him. "She needs a pick-me-up, or we'll never make it to the top."

Uncle Ned grimaces. "She needs more than just a pick-me-up. And if she's this bad off already, she's in no shape to keep going."

"But we can't stop," you protest. "Everything depends on our success. It's a matter of life or death."

"No, it isn't—not yet, anyway. Zoey's finished up here, and I need you to keep an eye on her. Take her back to Camp Four."

"But Uncle Ned—"

"Sorry, Zach, but I don't want to hear it. This is your sister's life. It isn't worth risking."

He turns and marches away, and you know that you no longer have a choice.

A moment later, Nawa finds you. "We go down," he says. "I help you."

Together, you and Nawa bring your sister safely down the mountain and into your tent at Camp Four. You'll move farther down as soon as you are able.

"I'm so sorry," Zoey tells you, when she finally catches her breath.

You shake your head. "It's not your fault, Zo. It's mine. If I had made better choices, I could've helped you. And we'd be on our way to the summit right now."

Instead, your Mount Everest expedition is a failure. Tears well in your eyes as you silently ask yourself what's next. Your family will be left with nothing.

So what's after Everest? You suppose your parents will need to find a cheap place to live.

Turn to page 67.

You slide your backpack off your shoulders and dig into its contents. Near the bottom, you find what you were looking for: a miniature flag that bears your school's green, black and white emblem.

"Go, Arrows," you say, planting the flag into the rainbow of other ornaments that pepper the mountaintop.

Zoey smiles and pats your back. "Great, now let's get some pictures."

Turn to page 54.

You shake your head at Nawa. "No, I can't do this without you."

"We come right back," Nawa promises.

You angrily grab Nawa's arm. "My uncle said take care of us," you shout over the storm. "We all go together!"

Nawa stares at you for a moment. His eyes tell you he wants to argue. But at last he bows slightly, signaling his agreement. You help Zoey slowly to her feet, and then the four of you trudge into the blinding storm.

Turn to page 36.

4

TOP OF THE WORLD

At last your turn arrives. You watch impatiently as Leslie Quaid fumbles with her harness. Nawa tries to help her clip onto the fixed rope, but she bats him away.

She's no bigger than Zoey, but her feisty temper is as red as her hair, and it puts Zoey's stubbornness to shame. Nawa looks at you and shrugs. Finally, Leslie clips on and begins her climb.

Nawa clips on next. You glance toward Zoey. She's stomping her feet and clapping her gloved hands together, trying to ward off frostbite. You wait for Nawa to begin his climb, then you clip onto the rope. Your stomach flips. This is it: the final push to the summit.

The rope looks ancient, like it's always been part of the mountain. You give it a good tug, just to make sure it'll hold. You dig in and start your climb up the Hillary Step.

You suddenly realize why everyone ahead of you is moving so slowly. Your pack feels like an elephant on your back. Your body seems disconnected from your brain;

your brain tells your foot to move, but the signal seems frozen in place. It takes forever just to move a step. Yet you continue upward. The rock wall is only 40 feet tall, but your climb seems to last an hour.

Finally, you haul yourself over the top of the Hillary Step, gasping for air you don't have. You unclip from the fixed rope and look ahead toward the summit. People are already posing for photos up there. It's not far now—and no more climbing. It's just 500 feet of walking, up a snowy slope, to the top.

You peer down the ice cliff. Zoey is climbing toward you, but her progress is painfully slow.

Ned joins you, putting a hand on your shoulder and shaking his head. "It's past our turnaround time," he says.

You check your watch. It's 1:18 p.m.

"I'm sorry," Ned continues, "but we need to go back."

"I can see the summit," you say. "We're almost there."

"Yes, Zach, but safety comes first. You know that."

In your heart, you know he's right. But even with your brain in a fuzz, you also know that you and Zoey need to reach the summit for your family. Are fortune and fame worth risking your life—and your sister's? What will you choose to do?

You know Uncle Ned well. If you protest hard enough, he'll change his mind. But you'll be risking your life and the lives of everyone else on your team.

Of course, if you turn back now, you have a much better chance of surviving Mount Everest's harsh reality. But there's no prize for being the youngest climber to "almost" reach the summit. You and your family will be left with nothing.

If you choose to change Uncle Ned's mind and keep climbing upward, turn to page 42.

If you choose to play it safe and start the trek downward, turn to page 60.

3
THE HILLARY STEP

Between you and the summit of Mount Everest lies one of the most dangerous stretches of your journey. It includes the Cornice Traverse (also known as the Knife Ridge because it's narrow like the sharp edge of a knife) and the Hillary Step.

Ned starts your team moving. You try to concentrate, but the thin air makes it harder and harder to think straight. You rattle your head to keep your brain alert; it doesn't help.

Ned leads you into a small, half-open tunnel of rock, ice and snow. You look back to make sure that Zoey is following closely. She's right there and gives you a little wave. Thank goodness your supplies could help her.

Up ahead, Nawa stands before the narrow traverse. One misstep to the right and he'll tumble 10,000 feet down the Kanshung Face. One misstep to the left and he'll fly 8,000 feet down the Southwest Face. He clips onto a fixed rope and continues on his way.

Now, it's your turn. You inch forward from the relative safety of the half-tunnel. You attach your harness onto the fixed rope with a sharp click, checking it twice before you start up the ridge. Zoey clips on behind you.

You feel a moment of panic. Your head swims. You've never felt the effect of heights like this before. As you slowly climb, you dig your crampons into the ridge at a sharp, crooked angle. Even over the wind's roar, you hear the crampons crunch into the ice-covered snow.

Suddenly, the snow beneath your right foot gives way. You lurch to the side and slide helplessly toward 10,000 feet of frozen, jagged rocks. There's nothing to grab; you're going to fall.

Snap!

The fixed rope jerks your harness to a stop, and you dangle. Your heart pounds, seemingly in your throat. Your fingers scramble for purchase on the ice until Nawa's strong hands pull you back to safety.

"Th-th-thanks," you stammer.

Nawa's kind eyes crinkle, and he breaks into a broad smile. "*Zolhamu*—how you say? Easy," he replies. He claps you on the back and resumes his climb.

Zoey throws her arms around you.

"Don't ever do that again," she orders. Her voice sounds tired and weak.

You breathe a shallow sigh of relief and follow your team upward.

You clear the Cornice Traverse. Ahead of you, the Hillary Step awaits. It's a 40-foot climb up a spur of snow and ice. It's also the last real obstacle before you and Zoey stand atop the tallest mountain in the world.

Unfortunately, it's the last stretch for other teams too. As you reach the base of the Hillary Step, you find a bottleneck of people. Other teams of climbers are already clipped onto the fixed rope and scaling—one at a time— up to the summit. There's a line waiting at the bottom, and you're at the end of it.

You watch the climbers impatiently. Thanks to them, you're stuck here, standing still. You feel the cold start to grip you. Why are the climbers moving so slowly?

You check your watch. It's nearly 1:00 p.m.—the time Uncle Ned said you'd have to turn around and go back. You look at Zoey. She's huddled next to Nawa, and she's in rough shape. She mumbles something, but you don't understand her.

Altitude sickness is taking her fast. If you don't make the climb to the summit now, Zoey might never get there.

Fortunately, there is an option. Who says you have to wait? You've climbed around people before. All you have to do is clip onto the fixed line and start moving. Whenever someone gets in your way, you just clip off the line and loop around. Once you've passed them, you clip back onto the line and continue up.

So should you wait in line for your turn? Or should you make the climb now? What will you choose to do?

The longer you wait, the harder the climb will be. You and Zoey are getting colder and losing energy by the second. If you climb now, you'll have a better chance of making it. Plus, Uncle Ned made it very clear that 1:00 p.m. is the turnaround time—and the clock is ticking.

However, passing climbers is dangerous. If you fall when you're clipped off, there's no rope to catch you. There's nothing to keep you from plummeting to your doom.

If you choose to climb now, turn to page 56.

If you choose to wait in line, turn to page 41.

6
LOST

The storm explodes into a full-out blizzard. You crawl slowly down the mountain with Zoey, Nawa and Jigmi. The swirling wind howls and tears at your gear. Dark clouds surround you as the snow whips, forming ever-moving jagged walls of white. You can't see more than three feet ahead. The whirling snow confuses your sense of direction. Ned's faint trail is quickly erased.

You jump and stumble over rocks hidden beneath the shifting snow. A few more lurching steps and you realize you've lost the trail. You whirl around in a panic, looking for Zoey and the Sherpas.

Through the blinding blizzard, you glimpse Nawa's red cap against the darkened sky. Zoey and Jigmi fade into view behind him, and you breathe a sigh of relief.

But your relief doesn't last long; you're still lost. Are you near the Balcony? Are you a long way from it? Have you already passed it? Your mind won't focus, and it is impossible to see any landmarks around you.

Nawa steps close and yells over the wind, "You and sister wait here!" He gestures toward Jigmi. "We find trail! Then we come for you!"

You barely hear him, but you understand. Is this a good idea? Can you keep your sister safe on your own? Will the Sherpas come back for you? Or should you demand that the four of you stick together, no matter what happens? What will you choose to do?

If you don't get back on the trail, you could wander, lost, until you freeze to death. The Sherpas are your best chance to find your way again. And if they go it alone, they'll find the trail much more quickly—and speed equals survival.

However, a lot can go wrong up here. If your sister takes a turn for the worse or if you become injured, you might not be able to handle the situation alone. Besides, the altitude is making you paranoid; you're worried that the Sherpas won't come back for you.

If you choose to let them go, turn to page 50.

If you choose to have them stay, turn to page 17.

"Is there anything that can help her?" you cry.

Nawa digs and digs. Eventually, he dumps the backpack onto the snow, searching for anything that might save your sister. He looks up at you and shakes his head.

Tears well in your eyes, but you feel the moisture crystallize. The tears crunch as you blink them away.

"Then you have to help me," you order. "We need to get Zoey to Camp Four." You try to pick her up, but you succeed only in dragging her a few feet.

Nawa and Jigmi rush to your aid. With their help, you are able to stand your sister upright. But she offers no support; her body remains limp. After a few steps, the four of you tumble into the snow. You again try to lift your sister. Nawa just stares at you.

"Come on!" you scream.

Nawa shakes his head. "Too dangerous."

He stands and tries to guide you away from Zoey.

You shove him. "I'm not leaving her!"

Nawa remains patient and gentle. "So sorry, Zach. Zoey die soon. We must go, or we die too."

As if in response to his words, the light around you suddenly shifts. Everything goes dark, as if someone flipped off a switch. You look up and see that the brilliant sun is being quickly covered by dark clouds, rolling up from below. The weather is changing from beautiful to deadly, and the storm is moving from the bottom up.

Your heart feels as if someone is squeezing it. Your body convulses. You let out a loud, terrible cry. The storm means the end of all hope for your sister. Even in good weather, getting her down the mountain in time would be difficult. Moving her through a storm like this will be impossible, which means you have to do the unthinkable. You have to leave her behind.

Turn to page 38.

5
THE DESCENT

Ned gathers your group. "Don't let your guard down," he says. "This is one of the most dangerous times in our climb. Most accidents happen on the way down. Watch out for each other. Got it?"

You notice Leslie looking off in the distance. Will fumbles with his gloves. You wonder if they're even paying attention. But then, you feel your own thoughts slipping away too.

Out of the corner of your eye, you see a white rabbit—a snow hare—bounding over the edge of a drift. You have the strangest urge to jump after it. You shake your head and bite the inside of your cheek. You're seeing things; snow hares don't live on Mount Everest. And up here, following a white rabbit will get you a one-way ticket straight to Wonderland.

Turn to the next page.

Minute by tortured minute, you descend back toward the Hillary Step, with Ned leading the way. You follow Zoey; she's moving slower than ever. Will, Leslie, Kenji and Fetang all pass you. Nawa and Jigmi stay back with you and Zoey, most likely at the request of Uncle Ned.

You catch up to Zoey. "You doing okay?" you ask.

"I'm fine, Mom," she mumbles. "Ready in a few."

Mom? She called you *Mom*? You grab Zoey's jacket and stop her progress. She tries to bat you away.

"Zoey," you yell. "Focus!"

Through her goggles, you see her eyes blink rapidly. You pinch her arm as hard as you can through the layers.

"Ow! What—? Zach!" Zoey snaps back to herself for a moment. But then she slurs, "I'm so tired."

"I know, Zo. But we have to keep going."

Nawa climbs over to you and asks, "She okay?"

"I think so," you reply.

You hope so.

You stick close to Zoey all the way to the Hillary Step. The rest of your group has already made the descent down the fixed rope. You ensure that Zoey's harness is clipped onto the rope, and then she starts her rappel down the rocky, icy face.

Your muscles tremble as you make your own descent. Blackness crowds the edges of your vision. You fight through it, and you make it to the bottom.

When you get there, Zoey is still clipped onto the rope, slumped to the side, face down in the snow.

You unclip yourself and Zoey. You quickly flip her over. "Zoey!" you yell.

She doesn't respond. She's barely breathing.

You sling your pack to the ground just as Nawa and Jigmi join you. You point to the pack, too desperate to speak. Nawa seems to understand and opens your pack. "What find?" he asks, pawing through the contents.

If you have a Dex shot, turn to page 51.

If you do not have a Dex shot, turn to page 28.

It's 10:55 p.m. You and Zoey crawl out of your tent and finish gearing up. You pull on the outer layer of your coat and your double-layer cap. You fix crampons to your boots, and you check the flow of oxygen into your mask. You shrug your heavy pack onto your shoulders.

Above you, the stars are so bright and clear that you feel as if you could touch them. Behind you, a cluster of small, flapping yellow tents dot the landscape. On your right, a bizarre graveyard of oxygen canisters adds to the strange setting. The rocky landscape of Camp Four could just as well be the moon.

"I feel like Darth Vader with a Wookiee on my back," you tell Zoey.

She grins behind her mask.

Uncle Ned gathers your team of nine: you, Zoey, Will Owens, Leslie Quaid, Kenji Sherpa, Fetang Sherpa, Jigmi Sherpa and Nawa Sherpa. The wind tugs at your jacket, and you feel a sudden sense of loneliness. The weight of what you're about to attempt presses onto your shoulders. It takes away what little breath you have.

Zoey seems to sense your uneasiness; she punches your arm lightly. You don't feel so alone after all.

"We turn around at 1:00 p.m. No later," orders Ned.

The air is thin up here. With his oxygen mask off, Ned strains to breathe. He looks at each of you in turn and waits to see you nod in agreement.

After you do, he slides his oxygen mask back into place. Then Ned leads the way as you begin your final ascent to the top.

Turn to page 44.

Progress is slow. Your body aches, switching between the burning sensation of tired muscles and a coldness unlike any other. You're still not sure where you are, and you—and especially Zoey—are slowing the Sherpas.

You are forced to stop. Zoey is only a few feet behind you, but in this storm, that almost puts her out of sight. You wait for your sister to close the gap, then you turn to start again.

The Sherpas are gone.

"Nawa! Jigmi!" you shout.

You are answered only by the wind's unending roar.

You hurry forward, frantic. "Nawa! Jigmi! Are you there? Where are you?"

You look through the storm, desperate to see Nawa's red cap again. Snow whistles and screams around you; Nawa remains invisible. The cold finds its way into your heavy jacket and gloves, and you shudder.

Panic grips you, and it makes you careless. You focus only on the Sherpas. You stop paying attention to anything else, like the mountain.

The snow beneath your left foot gives, and you slip. You tumble into the snow, and suddenly you're sliding. You flail wildly, unable to find any footing. Your hands grasp a rocky ledge just as your body slips over it. You are left hanging at the edge of a cliff.

The muscles in your arms burn like fire. You feel them cracking and tearing as you struggle to hold on. But all too soon, the pain becomes too much to bear. You cannot hold on any longer, so you do the only thing you can.

You let go.

For a moment, you are falling. The mountain zips past your eyes, and you hear the beginning of a scream. But that noise is cut off by a loud *thunk*. It is the last sound you ever hear.

Turn to page 67.

The storm explodes into a full-out blizzard. You crawl slowly down the mountain with Nawa and Jigmi. The swirling wind howls and tears at your gear. Dark clouds surround you as the snow whips, forming ever-moving jagged walls of white. You can't see more than three feet ahead. The whirling snow confuses your sense of direction. Ned's faint trail is quickly being erased.

You jump and stumble over rocks hidden beneath the shifting snow. A few more lurching steps and you realize that you've lost the trail. Are you near the Balcony? Are you a long way from it? Have you already passed it? Your mind won't focus, and it's impossible to see any landmarks around you.

Nawa steps close and yells over the wind, "We find trail! You follow!"

Everything after that is confusion. Hours pass. Your mind continually drifts to memories of your sister. You can't believe she's gone. You can't believe you left her!

You follow Nawa and Jigmi as they weave through the blinding whiteness. You half walk, half stumble down the mountain. Your mind doesn't register time anymore. You think of nothing except Zoey.

You see the fixed ropes that will lead you down a final descent to the flat and rocky South Col.

You're tired, and the short rappel down the ice bulge seems overwhelming. But somehow, you make it. Your crampons crunch onto Camp Four's level ground. You pick out the tent that you and Zoey shared an eon ago. You lurch toward your tent, rip open the zipper and then collapse inside.

You see Zoey's stuff, and reality slaps you in the face. Your sister is gone, dead—and it's your fault. If you had made better choices, your sister would be alive right now. Instead, you will live the rest of your life knowing that she died chasing your dangerous dream.

Turn to page 67.

You reach into your bag and pull out a canister of oxygen. "Here, I think this will help," you tell your sister. You attach the second canister to Zoey's mask. Then you open the valve further, so she's getting more air than she was before.

"I'm cranking it up a notch," you explain. "It will give you better airflow."

Through Zoey's mask, you see alertness sneak back into her eyes. Her torso straightens, her arms and legs flex—life returns to her. Your idea has worked.

Her eyes meet yours, and you read gratitude in them. But her grateful expression quickly shifts into one of deep concern.

"Won't I run out of oxygen?" she asks.

You shake your head. "This is extra. Besides, what good is it to save the oxygen for later? You need it now, and we have a mountain to conquer."

Zoey shrugs and says, "I guess you're right."

Turn to page 21.

You've already climbed higher than ever before. The thin air is taking its toll on your sister and you. It isn't just unwise to clip off the line; it's foolish. You decide to wait your turn.

But as the minutes tick by—as your watch inches closer to 1:00 p.m.—you begin to regret your decision. What if you run out of time? What if you miss your chance to fulfill your dream? What if your family is left with nothing?

You shudder, not from the cold but from the thought of losing everything.

Turn to page 18.

"Please, Uncle Ned, we're almost there," you plead. "Just a little longer. If it takes too long, we'll turn around. I promise."

The rest of your team joins in. Leslie Quaid and Will Owens echo your words. Like you and Zoey, they've paid a lot to be on this expedition. They want to reach the top as much as anyone.

Ned looks at his watch and sighs. "All right. Fine. We'll keep going. But if I say turn around, I mean it. No arguing. Got it?" He points toward the summit. "That, this mountain, isn't worth dying for. Agreed?" He looks pointedly at you and Zoey. You both nod.

The brief rest isn't enough to prepare you for the next leg of the climb. It's not too steep, but you still need your ice axe to keep steady. Each step seems to take more than a minute to complete. Your body aches, and your brain can't process what you're doing. Plus, every breath brings your oxygen canister closer to empty.

You look ahead and squint through the sun and the howling wind. You see a sharp, white edge on the horizon. One painful step at a time, the white edge inches closer.

Then you see Ned turn around and throw his arms skyward. Nawa smothers him with a bear hug. You drag yourself the final few steps, and you've made it. You're standing on top of the world, at 29,035 feet.

Prayer flags, photos and other colorful trinkets—things people left to prove they were here—are scattered everywhere, fluttering in the wind. The actual summit is only the size of a picnic table, and only a few of you can stand there at a time. But it seems like you can see across the continent. The sky goes on forever—a crystal blue.

Zoey grabs your arm and spins you around. You're so dizzy that you fall over, laughing.

Zoey falls beside you. "We made it, Zach," she gasps. "We really, really made it!"

If you brought your school flag, turn to page 16.

If you did not, turn to page 54.

2
GOING UP

You move upward, single file, no one speaking. Ned leads the line, making sure the ropes are securely fixed to the ice. Kenji helps him. Leslie Quaid follows Kenji, then Nawa. You're behind Nawa, watching his bright red cap bob through the frigid night. You feel alone, even with Zoey right behind you and Nawa not far ahead. But that's okay; it's not a lonely kind of alone. It allows you to think, to really enjoy what you're doing. Fetang, Will Owens and Jigmi trail Zoey at the rear of the line.

Inside your oxygen mask, your breath sounds loud and strained. You wonder if the mask is making it harder to breathe. You lift it from your face for a moment. Your head instantly spins; you stumble; your lungs scream for air. Zoey catches up to you and slaps your mask back into place.

"What are you thinking?" she scolds.

"I don't know," you say truthfully. With the flow of oxygen, your head clears. It's just a moment after you've done it, but you can't imagine why you would remove your mask. You give Zoey a quick smile. "Thanks, Zo."

Nawa turns around, and you give him a thumbs-up to let him know you're okay. And so the climb continues.

Ahead of you, a lighted squiggle moves up a dark wall. It takes you a moment to realize it, but you are seeing another team of climbers making their own attempt for the summit.

The moon moves above the peak of Makalu, another mountain in the range. The snow beneath your boots suddenly glows with an unearthly light. Ned sends a message back along the line of climbers: "Turn off your headlamps. There's plenty of light from the moon—no need to waste your batteries."

The climb is steep and slippery. You dig your crampons into the ice with each step, driving home your ice axe to help you hang on. You make sure to clip your harness into the ropes Uncle Ned has secured. Without the ropes, one wrong step could send you sliding off the edge of the mountain.

Your body aches with cold, and you're more tired than you've ever been before. But you feel like you're on top of the world—because you almost are.

But soon, the bitter winds begin to take their toll. Each breath comes with a wheeze, and your head starts to throb. Hours pass, and each icy step becomes harder than the last. You grit your teeth and bear it. It's then that you see a thin line of blue light in the east: the sunrise!

Uncle Ned stops, signaling that it's time for a rest. You must have made it all the way to the Balcony, the small platform where climbers usually rest before reaching the South Summit, a peak below the main summit.

Everyone collapses in relief, even the Sherpas. You plop onto the ground, next to your sister. Her knees are drawn up, under her chin. You can't see her eyes through her goggles.

"Are you okay?" you ask.

For a moment, you think Zoey didn't hear you. But then she nods twice, as if speaking is too much effort.

The sun rises a little bit higher, and light explodes over the neighboring peaks. It seems like you can see the edge of the world in every direction. The spectacular views renew your energy. Your quaking muscles calm, and your head stops pounding. You wiggle your toes and stomp your boots on the ground. Despite your good mood, frostbite is digging in with its sharp, frozen teeth.

Everyone changes to a fresh canister of oxygen. Ned helps Zoey. Her shaking hands fumble with the straps. Ned leans close to talk with her. You cannot hear what they say. The howling wind scatters their words. Zoey shakes her head in a way you've seen many times before. It means she's arguing. And when Zoey argues, she almost always wins.

Ned stands back and looks at Zoey, as if considering something. Finally he nods, and Zoey gives you a weak thumbs-up.

The line forms again, and you inch your way toward the South Summit, another 1,000 feet up. Your lungs scream for more air. Your legs beg for rest. Each finger feels like a swollen slab of ice. Somehow, you keep going.

You focus straight ahead, following Nawa's red cap. Each time you glance backward, Zoey seems farther from you. You can't tell if she's slowing down or if what you're seeing is just a trick of the mountain's thin air. Your thoughts feel fuzzy around the edges.

Your exhausted group finally crowds onto a small plateau no bigger than your family's dining room table. It's the South Summit—28,700 feet high. And there, just around the corner, you see the summit of Mount Everest.

It's so close; you feel like you can almost reach out and touch the white-capped peak. You are only a couple of hours away from your family's bright future.

Zoey tugs on your sleeve and pulls you aside. Under her goggles and oxygen mask, her face is deathly white.

"I don't think I can make it," she gasps. "I'm so dizzy." Tears form in her eyes and instantly freeze.

Your heart sinks. "We're almost there, Zo. Just hang on," you say.

"I don't know if I can," she answers. "I need a boost."

A boost? That gives you an idea. Maybe one of your supplies can help her. You swing your pack to the ground and rifle through it with thick, clumsy fingers. Did you choose to bring something that can help Zoey?

If you brought extra oxygen, turn to page 40.

If not, but you brought hot tea, turn to page 68.

If not, but you brought a Dex shot, turn to page 62.

If you brought none of these, turn to page 14.

You nod. "Be careful, Nawa," you tell him, patting his shoulder. "We're counting on you."

The Sherpa pulls a long rope out of his pack, ties it around his waist, and hands the other end to you. "No let go," he warns. "This lead us back."

His gesture gives you an idea. Maybe there's something in your pack that can help the Sherpas.

If you brought a compass, turn to page 86.

If not, but you brought a GPS, turn to page 130.

If not, but you brought a rope, turn to page 118.

If you brought none of these, turn to page 95.

"Find the Dex shot," you tell Nawa.

Uncle Ned said it was a last resort, and this is looking very *last resort* to you.

Nawa digs out the syringe and hands it to you. You catch it in one hand, then transfer it to your teeth while you yank at Zoey's outer gear. You expose the skin of her hip enough to jam the shot into her.

"Sorry, Zo," you mutter. You press the plunger and pray for a miracle. You know that dexamethasone can take hours to work, but you don't have hours. You don't even have minutes.

Zoey groans, and it is the most beautiful sound you've ever heard.

You give her a shake. "Come on, Zo. Come back."

Her eyes open, and she focuses on your face. "Zach? Quit shaking me," she says.

You grin at Nawa and Jigmi. "She's going to be all right," you tell them.

The three of you help Zoey to her feet. She rubs her hip. "What did you do? Use a spear to give me that shot?"

You laugh, happy that she's okay—at least, for now.

Your group of four continues down the mountain. You can tell that Zoey is still struggling, but she's trying

not to show it. Your own breath comes in shallow, ragged gasps. Once or twice you think you see the white rabbit again. You remind yourself that it isn't real.

At last, you settle into a rhythm as your crampons bite into the ice and snow. Step, axe, breathe, breathe. Step, axe, breathe, breathe. Your progress downward is slow but steady.

Suddenly, the light around you shifts. Everything goes dark, as if someone flipped off a switch. You look up and see that the brilliant sun is being quickly covered by dark clouds, rolling up from below. The weather is changing from beautiful to deadly, and the storm is moving from the bottom up. You're heading right into the worst of it.

Turn to page 26.

Leslie Quaid digs a camera from her pack and begins snapping photos all around. She waves you and Zoey to her. You help Zoey to her feet with some difficulty. She's not moving very well. The two of you hobble over, and Leslie takes your picture. She hands the camera to Will Owens, who is grinning widely. He snaps several shots of Leslie then photographs the rest of your group. Will offers to take pictures of you and Zoey with your camera, too. You and your sister pose at the top of the world.

Nawa slaps you on the back. "You make it!" he says. "Easy as *chik, nyi, sum*—how you say—one, two, three?"

"Sure, Nawa, easy," you laugh.

Uncle Ned grabs you and Zoey in a tight hug. "You did it. I can't tell you how proud I am." He smiles brightly and then quickly moves to congratulate Leslie and Will.

Kenji, Nawa, Fetang and Jigmi chat in their native Sherpa language, probably about the descent. You see them pointing back the way you came. You glance at your watch, and a new chill runs through your body. It's nearly two hours after Uncle Ned's original turnaround time.

You've celebrated too long.

Turn to page 30.

You look at your watch again, and you look at Zoey. Frustrated, you shake your head. Too much is at stake; there isn't time to wait.

You grab your sister's hand and say, "Come on." You yank her forward, weaving your way around the men and women between you and the Hillary Step.

"What are we doing?" Zoey asks. Her voice sounds slightly slurred.

"We're running out of time," you explain. "So we're going up—now."

Zoey's head slowly tilts upward as she scans the wall of ice and snow. "What about those people? How will we get past them?"

The fixed line is clogged with climbers, many of whom almost seem frozen in place. They are blocking your path.

"The same way as always," you reply, trying to sound casual. "We'll just clip off and scoot around them."

Zoey's eyes lock onto yours; you read fear in them.

"I don't think this is a good idea," she tells you.

"Come on, Zo. We've climbed without fixed ropes before. Mom and dad are counting on us. We have to reach the summit."

You clip onto the fixed rope. "Are you with me?"

Zoey hesitates, but eventually she nods. She clips on behind you, and you're ready to go.

The rope looks ancient, like it's always been part of the mountain. You give it a good tug, just to make sure it'll hold. You dig in and start your climb up the Hillary Step.

You suddenly realize why everyone ahead of you is moving so slowly. Your pack feels like an elephant on your back. Your body seems disconnected from your brain; your brain tells your foot to move, but the signal seems stuck. It takes forever just to go one step.

Yet you continue upward.

Your first obstacle comes about 10 feet up the Hillary Step. Fortunately, you're high enough now that even if Uncle Ned notices you he can't stop you.

You look down at Zoey and shout above the wind, "Are you ready? Watch me! I'll clip off; you do exactly what I do!"

Zoey nods.

You unhook yourself from the fixed line and climb carefully to your right. You move slowly, doing your best to ensure your safety. You can't afford any mistakes. If you slip now, it will be the end of you.

"Be careful!" shouts Zoey.

You glance at the climber above you. You've moved far enough to the side that he's now out of your way. All you need to do is climb past him and then back to the rope.

You do just that. Your arms burn. Your side aches. Your pack feels like it's pulling against you. But when you return to the fixed rope and clip back onto it, you breathe a deep sigh of relief.

You turn to watch Zoey, and you hold your breath. She climbs more slowly and deliberately than you did. It takes her far longer to get around the climber, but she makes it back to you, and you greet her with a hug.

The two of you continue up the Hillary Step. Your next obstacle comes minutes later. You're only six or eight feet past the first climber when you come upon a second.

You clip off and shout another reminder to your sister. "Watch me! Do what I do!"

Again you slide to the right, and again you notice how badly your body aches from the effort. Your heavy backpack works against you, but this time the blowing wind seems to catch it, pulling it back harder than ever.

The snow beneath your left foot gives, and you slip. You cling to your climbing axe with both hands, kicking at the wall with your legs, trying to find a perch.

You hear Zoey scream, "Zach!"

Her cry fuels the panic growing within you. You flail wildly, unable to find any footing. Your hands begin to slip, and you know you're in trouble.

The muscles in your arms burn like fire. You feel them cracking and tearing as you struggle to hold on. But all too soon, the pain becomes too much to bear. You cannot hold on any longer, so you do the only thing you can.

You let go.

For a moment, you are falling. The mountain zips past your eyes, and you hear the beginning of a scream. But that noise is cut off by a loud *thunk*. It is the last sound you ever hear.

Turn to page 67.

You love your sister, and you respect the others on your team. You won't gamble their lives for any reward.

"Zoey is starting to struggle," you tell your uncle. "I might need help getting her back to Camp Four."

Uncle Ned nods and pats your shoulder. "This is the right choice," he says. "I'll get Nawa to help you."

He turns and marches away. You don't envy him, as you watch him share the bad news with the rest of your team. You see him point to his watch, and you can feel the heartbreak of each member as they realize their dream has been quashed.

A moment later, Nawa finds you. "We go down," he says. "I help you."

Turn to the next page.

Together, you and Nawa bring your sister safely down the mountain and into your tent at Camp Four. You'll move farther down as soon as you are able.

"I'm so sorry," Zoey tells you, when she finally catches her breath.

You shake your head. "It's my fault, Zo. If I had made better choices, maybe we'd be on our way to the summit right now."

Instead, your Mount Everest expedition is a failure. Tears well in your eyes as you silently ask yourself what's next. Your family will be left with nothing.

So what's after Everest? You suppose your parents will need to find a cheap place to live.

Turn to page 67.

You reach into your bag and pull out your Dex shot. "Here, I think this will help," you tell your sister. You get ready to administer the shot, but Uncle Ned interrupts, grabbing you by the wrist.

"What do you think you're doing?" barks your uncle.

"Zoey is really struggling," you tell him. "She needs a pick-me-up, or we'll never make it to the top."

Uncle Ned snatches the shot out of your hand. "Are you crazy? This isn't a toy. This is dexamethasone! It's not something you give someone casually. It's a last resort. It's a matter of life or death."

"But this is life or death," you protest.

"No, this is climbing a mountain. If Zoey's moving toward a point where she really will need this, then the answer is simple. She's finished up here, and I need you to stay with her. Take her back to Camp Four, and wait for the rest of us there."

"But Uncle Ned—"

"Sorry, Zach, but I don't want to hear it. This is your sister's life. It isn't worth risking."

He turns and marches away, and you know that you no longer have a choice.

A moment later, Nawa finds you. "We go down," he says. "I help you."

Together, you and Nawa bring your sister safely down the mountain and into your tent at Camp Four. You'll move farther down as soon as you are able.

"I'm so sorry," Zoey tells you, when she finally catches her breath.

You shake your head. "It's not your fault, Zo. It's mine. If I had made better choices, I could've helped you. And we'd be on our way to the summit right now."

Instead, your Mount Everest expedition is a failure. Tears well in your eyes as you silently ask yourself what's next. Your family will be left with nothing.

So what's after Everest? You suppose your parents will need to find a cheap place to live.

Turn to page 67.

Choose four of the following items. Mark your choices so you remember what's in your pack. But be careful: The items you bring might mean the difference between life and death.

__ **Batteries:** You have a fresh set of batteries in your headlamp, but you're not sure how long they'll last. Running out of light could pose a real danger.

__ **Compass:** If you get lost or separated from the rest of your team, this may be the only thing that keeps you on track.

__ **Crampon repair kit:** The crampons on your boots are sharp and ready to go. But if one should break, you'll need to fix it in order to continue climbing.

__ **"Dex" shot:** Some climbers choose to carry a syringe of dexamethasone. It's a powerful medicine that can temporarily offset the effects of mountain sickness.

__ **Extra Gloves:** You will be wearing a heavy-duty pair of climbing gloves, but an extra pair—especially in this harsh, high altitude—never hurts.

__ **Extra oxygen:** Right now, there are enough canisters of oxygen for everyone on your team. But if the climb takes too long, you may need an extra boost.

__ **GPS:** If you get lost or separated from the rest of your team, this item will tell you exactly where you are and what path you should take.

__ **Rope:** Whether you are climbing Mount Everest or hiking through the woods, this handy and versatile item can do a lot for you.

__ **School flag:** Many climbers put their country's flag at the summit. Your math teacher promised no home-work for a year if you leave your school flag at the top.

__ **Thermos of hot tea:** Dehydration is a real threat when climbing. You are already bringing two liters of hot water, but more hot tea could keep you energized.

After you've made your choices, turn to page 33.

THE END

TRY AGAIN

You reach into your bag and pull out your thermos of hot tea. "Here, I think this will help," you tell your sister. You twist off the lid, flip it upside down and pour the steaming liquid into it.

"The hot tea will warm you from the inside out," you explain. "But drink slowly."

You help Zoey lift her oxygen mask, and you guide the lid to her lips. She takes three quick sips. You slide the mask back into place, allowing her to get the air she needs. Then you repeat the process.

Soon, the lid is nearly empty. You see alertness sneak back into Zoey's eyes. Her torso straightens, her arms and legs flex—life returns to her. Your idea has worked.

Zoey's eyes meet yours, and you read gratitude in them. But her grateful expression quickly shifts into one of deep concern.

"Won't you need this tea later?" she asks.

You shake your head. "What good does it do to save it? You need it now, and we have a mountain to conquer."

Zoey shrugs and says, "I guess you're right."

Turn to page 21.

8

ON THE MOVE

As you wait, one of the climbers stands and wanders away from the huddle. To your surprise, she starts taking off her gear. Her fingertips are black with frostbite.

"What are . . . you doing?" you stammer.

Her response is a low moan.

The blue climber, still the strongest of the group, herds her back and helps her put on her gear again. She slides onto her side and curls into the snow.

A moment later, you begin to wonder if that really just happened. Strange visions make it hard to know if you're dreaming or awake.

You're on Mount Everest. But then your ice axe is a baseball bat. You're standing at home plate, on a field, ready to swing. The grass is a deep, emerald green. Zoey stands before you, about to hurl a pitch. But she's not wearing a glove—why isn't she wearing her glove?

No matter. You're warm. And comfortable. And ready to fall into a deep sleep.

Smack!

Something hits your face—hard. The baseball scene disappears, and you're left lying in the snow on a deadly slope of Mount Everest.

You stare up at the blue climber, who's leaning over you with his fist clenched. Your ice-filled brain registers that he must have hit you in order to wake you. He offers his hand and pulls you up to sitting.

"Thanks," you shout.

"I thought we lost you," the blue climber yells back. "You could have died!"

You know he's right. Listening to someone say it aloud makes your skin crawl—or it would, if your skin didn't already feel frozen to your bones.

Afraid to fall asleep, you feel an urge to get moving. You anxiously wait, staring into the hypnotic swirl of snow. Time passes, and you wonder if the storm will ever lighten up.

You hear the answer before you see it. The wind's roar softens slightly. You look around, and you can finally see a couple of the nearby peaks. The storm is still ferocious, but the clouds have lifted just enough; your visibility is better than it's been since you left the summit. And based on those peaks, you're confident that you know where you are and where you need to go.

You turn to tell Zoey the good news. Your mouth falls wide open. Her gloves are gone, and her fingertips are black with frostbite—just like the other climber's were. Or, worse yet, you start to think maybe Zoey was that other climber. The fact that she's untied herself from the short rope strengthens your suspicion.

You mentally run through the list of items you packed; it's hard to focus. Did you bring extra gloves?

If you brought extra gloves, turn to page 116.

If you didn't bring extra gloves, turn to page 100.

Your last shred of energy is gone, whipped away by Mount Everest's dark, stormy winds. Your mind may be running at half speed, but it's working enough to know that you can't make it back to Camp Four. Your only chance at survival is to wait and hope for rescue.

You, Zoey and the other climbers gather as closely together as possible. The storm shrieks and screams around you, battering at your backs with icy fists. You can only sit and wonder if you made the right choice.

Turn to page 131.

You and Zoey huddle together for warmth. You're alone, near the top of Mount Everest, in a blizzard; you've never felt so small and afraid. You feel your body shutting down. Your eyes flutter closed.

Zoey begins thrashing and clawing at her oxygen mask. Your eyes snap open, and you try to calm her. She looks wild, and her face is covered in frost. Then, suddenly, Zoey slumps in your arms, unconscious.

Her oxygen must have run out. You set Zoey on the ground and dig frantically through your pack. You find nothing that can help.

You rake through Zoey's pack and again find nothing useful. Your fingers are frozen—they don't feel attached to your hands anymore. You fumble with Zoey's oxygen gauge. It reads empty.

You check Zoey. She's barely breathing.

You fling your own oxygen canister to the ground and check the gauge: less than a quarter full.

You look through the storm, desperate to see Nawa's red cap again. Snow whistles and screams around you; Nawa remains invisible. The cold finds its way into your heavy jacket and gloves, and you shudder.

It's then that you notice: You've let go of the rope.

You scramble on your hands and knees, but the rope is nowhere in sight. With dread, you realize the Sherpas will never be able to find you in this weather. They aren't coming back. You and Zoey are on your own.

You still have a little oxygen left. You can share it with your sister, or you can keep it for yourself. What will you choose to do?

The two of you are alone, and that means it's up to you to get Zoey back safely. You'll need your strength to help her down the mountain. Keeping all of your oxygen will ensure that you maximize your strength.

If you share your oxygen with Zoey, you'll be weaker for it. However, she may be revived enough to continue the descent, and you won't have to do all of the work. But will there be enough oxygen for both of you?

If you choose to keep your oxygen for yourself, turn to page 106.

If you choose to share your oxygen with Zoey, turn to page 128.

"We wait," you yell above the wind's roar. To further emphasize your decision, you point toward the ground.

The blue climber nods and then slides closer to you. You pull your legs to your chest, tuck your head between your knees and wrap your arms around your body. This position offers little protection against the wind and snow, but every bit helps.

One by one, each member of the group joins you in a tiny huddle in the snow. You sit snuggly between the blue climber and your sister. Your other three companions form the rest of a small circle—and in that circle you wait, silently praying for the storm to end.

Turn to page 69.

If there's one thing that was hammered into your memory during training, it's to trust your compass. Even if your mind isn't always sharp, that compass needle is. You shake off your doubts and angle your steps to the left.

Your headlamp's beam picks up a writhing, red snake. You cry out and jump back.

"It's not real," you tell yourself. "It can't be." But the snake doesn't disappear.

After a moment's pause, you discover that it is indeed real—but it's not a snake. It's a fixed rope whipping in the wind. This rope will lead you up the mountain.

You clip your harness onto the rope and start your steep climb up the icy face, one agonizing step at a time. The rope keeps your feet on track, but you find it harder than ever to focus.

Eventually, you reach the end of the fixed rope. You clip off and stumble your way up a more gradual slope. You walk seemingly for hours, until huge shapes appear at the edges of your headlamp. You've made it to the shale outcroppings where you and Leslie left the group. Zoey has to be near.

With shaking hands, you check your compass again. You angle a bit to the right. A few steps later, a swatch of blue catches your eye. With a cry, you rush forward as fast as your weary legs will take you. You've found the group.

The blue climber and two others huddle against an outcropping of rock, just where you left them. Another climber sits alone a few feet past them. No one moves or even seems to know you're there.

Zoey isn't the climber in the blue jacket, but she could be any one of the others. You push back the fuzziness in your brain and move to the climber to the right of the man in blue. You crouch close to her and peer into her goggles.

Not Zoey—not unless she's aged 30 years and changed her eye color to brown.

You try the next climber. Her eyes are closed, but the hair might be a match.

You shake the climber as hard as you can. "Zoey Anne Manning, you get up right now!" you shout.

You hear a small groan. The climber's eyes blink open, and she squints into your headlamp. It's Zoey, and she's awake—alive!

"Zach?" she mouths, although you do not hear a sound.

"I'm here, Zo."

You remember the oxygen in your pack. And although each movement feels like you're lifting an entire building,

you manage to attach a fresh canister for Zoey. You crawl to the blue climber and do the same.

The older person in the group is next. After her, you have one canister left. You can't make it to your feet, so you stay on your hands and knees. You drag the canister to the person huddled a few feet away.

His gloves lie beside his body, his oxygen mask next to them. His blackened face wears no goggles, and his eyes stare straight ahead. It's too late for this climber.

You choke back a sob and return to your sister. You're too tired to speak. You want to get up and run down the mountain with Zoey, but your body won't cooperate. Thankfully, the fresh oxygen seems to be helping her.

Perhaps if the two of you work together, you can make it back to Camp Four before you end up like the frozen climber. But even working together, you're not sure you can physically—or mentally—survive another climb. Maybe, if you wait it out and conserve your energy, you can last until a rescue team finds you. What will you choose to do?

If you leave now, you'll be saving precious, lifesaving time, and you've already seen what the mountain can do to a climber up here. If you wait for a possible rescue, you may be waiting for something that never comes.

However, a rescue may also be just a few minutes away. And if you leave now, you might exhaust yourselves to the point of death.

If you choose to leave now, turn to page 98.

If you choose to wait, turn to page 72.

If it weren't frozen, your heart would probably break. You turn your back on the four huddled climbers. You know it will probably be the last time you see them, and you don't even know their names.

You and Zoey half walk, half stumble down the mountain. Your mind doesn't register time anymore. You just know that the going is slow.

You almost cry when you see the fixed ropes that will lead you down a final descent to the flat and rocky South Col. You can't yet see the yellow tents, but you know they're close.

You're tired, and the short rappel down the ice bulge seems overwhelming. But somehow, the two of you make it. Your crampons crunch onto Camp Four's level ground. You pick out the tent that you and Zoey shared an eon ago. Zoey falls to her knees with a cry, and you help her up again. You lurch toward your tent, rip open the zipper and collapse inside.

You and Zoey have made it.

Turn to page 119.

10

A LONG, COLD NIGHT

Every movement seems to take forever. Your arms and legs feel as if they're filled with cement. Your strength is at its absolute breaking point, but you must carry on.

The blizzard has long since erased any tracks you could follow. You find yourself lost in a swirling mass of ice and snow. You pull a compass out of your pocket and squint at it in the dull light of your headlamp. The needle spins and rocks and finally lands in place.

According to the compass, you should veer to your left. But your instincts say that you came into camp from the other direction and that you should angle your path to the right.

You tap the compass and watch the needle go haywire. Maybe it's not even working. You feel confused, but you know you have to act fast. Right or left? Should you trust your instincts or the compass? What will you choose to do?

One of the qualities needed to conquer Mount Everest is an unshakable belief in yourself. You've got to have your wits about you and trust your instincts.

However, the high-altitude air plays tricks on your mind. Your thinking may not always be straight. The compass, if it's working, is much more reliable.

If you choose to follow your instincts and go to the right, turn to page 114.

If you choose to follow your compass and go to the left, turn to page 77.

You quickly tug the pack off your back and dig inside. "Here," you say to Nawa, "take this."

You hand him the compass, and then you blush. His look asks the question you're asking yourself. *Why didn't we use this sooner?*

You shrug, blaming it on the thin air affecting your ability to think clearly.

"Take it and go," you say to Nawa.

He bows in gratitude, and then the Sherpas disappear into the storm.

Turn to page 73.

"Won't leave you," you tell the climber. "Come on!"

He shakes his head again, tightly wrapping his arms around his body. Tucked together like that, he resembles a big, blue boulder. And up here, he might as well be one; you'll never move him on your own. Your only hope is to change his mind.

"You can't . . . give up," you say. "You'll . . . freeze."

He ignores you.

"Not just . . . yourself you'll be killing," you plead. "There are . . . three other climbers . . . counting on you."

Still, he does not stir.

An anger rises within you, one that momentarily warms your frozen core. You reach down and grab the blue climber, trying to shake some sense into him. You don't understand. You can't believe he's willing to give up. His life is at stake.

You continue shaking him, shouting, "Get up! Get up! Get up!"

He swats you away.

You won't quit on him. You can't. You grab him again, this time trying to pull him to his feet.

Again he swats you away, mumbling something that sounds like, "Leave me alone."

He isn't thinking clearly. His actions are not his own. No one in his right mind would decide to die on Everest, right after achieving a lifelong dream.

You approach him a third time. "I won't . . . let you die." You grab the blue climber, shaking and pulling with all of your might. "Don't you . . . understand? You'll die! I won't . . . let that happen!"

He seems to awaken, as if from a slumber. The blue climber unfolds himself and slowly rolls onto his knees.

"That's it," you say, clapping your hands in support. "You can do it."

It seems to take everything within him, and his movements are slow and staggered, but he eventually rises to his feet.

You slap him on the shoulder. "I knew you . . . wouldn't give up. Let's get the . . . others going."

You turn away from him. You feel his hands suddenly clasp your back. He yanks backward, nearly knocking you off your feet.

"I told you to leave me alone," he snarls.

The thin air is affecting his brain, so you can't blame him for what happens next. With surprising strength, he swings you to your left, and you slip. You tumble into the snow, and suddenly you're sliding. You flail wildly, unable to find any footing. Your hands grasp a rocky ledge just as your body slips over it. You are left hanging at the edge of a cliff.

The muscles in your arms burn like fire. You feel them cracking and tearing as you struggle to hold on. But all too soon, the pain becomes too much to bear. You cannot hold on any longer, so you do the only thing you can.

You let go.

For a moment, you are falling. The mountain zips past your eyes, and you hear the beginning of a scream. But that noise is cut off by a loud *thunk*. It is the last sound you ever hear.

Turn to page 67.

You unhook your canister and take off your mask. Your first breath of Everest's thin air feels like a thousand knives stabbing your lungs. You collapse into the snow, gasping, feeling as if you're drowning.

You don't know how long you stay there. But slowly you adjust, inhaling five quick breaths between each small movement. You crawl to Zoey and hook your oxygen canister to her mask. Then you cross your fingers, and you wait.

Turn to the next page.

Zoey gasps and her eyes open. "Zach?"

You grab your twin sister in a bear hug. "I . . . thought I'd . . . lost you."

"I remember Nawa and Jigmi leaving," she replies weakly. But then she bites her lip. "Are they coming back soon?"

"We have to . . . keep going. I don't . . . think . . . they're coming." Your words are stilted, cut off by short, gasping breaths.

Zoey lurches to a stand. She takes off her mask and hands it to you. She sways on her feet. You take a couple of breaths, then hand her mask back.

You and Zoey pick a direction, and you start down the mountain, into the heart of the storm.

Turn to page 108.

For the first moment in several hours, your sister's life is no longer in your hands. You become suddenly aware of how deeply tired you are. Every movement is a labor that takes several minutes to accomplish. You notice the hunger pangs in your stomach, but you are too weak even to look for food.

Your eyelids become too heavy to hold open. You fight against this weariness. You do not wish to sleep, not as long as your sister is in danger. However, it is a losing battle. You remain alert for as long as you can, but eventually you fall into a deep slumber.

By the time you awaken, the sun is shining brightly through the tent's walls. The air is eerily still. The storm has passed. You glance to your side, half hoping to see Zoey's face. Instead, Leslie Quaid stares back at you.

She begins to mumble a weak thank you, but you do not wait to hear it. You leap up and out of your tent. What you find is a war zone. Tents are ripped. Supplies are scattered. And a handful of wounded climbers wander across the camp like zombies.

The scene is evidence of the ordeal you've just been through. It is almost too much for your exhausted mind to bear. You feel light-headed. Your body sways back and forth. For a moment, you believe you will pass out. But you catch yourself, slowly coming back to your senses.

After that, your memories become hazy and blurred. You remember telling a group of climbers where you left Zoey and the others. You remember watching a team of rescuers ascend the mountain, even as another team leads you down.

You remember Camp Three. Camp Two. Camp One. Then Base Camp. You remember finding your parents there, and crying.

You remember the next day. And the next. And the next. And you remember your dad telling you Zoey and Uncle Ned are gone.

Memories are all you have left—memories and a haunting question: What would've happened if you had made a different choice?

Turn to page 67.

It's now or never. You know you can't wait to find Uncle Ned. The howling wind batters the walls of your little tent while you pack a compass and a few extra things to bring up the mountain. Leslie cries out in her sleep, and you feel bad leaving her alone. But Zoey needs you more—and she's your sister.

You exit the tent and make another quick stop, raking through your team's pile of oxygen canisters. You say a silent "thank you" to the Sherpas who brought them up the mountain. Then, checking the gauges to ensure that the canisters are full, you stuff them into your pack.

Turn to page 84.

You consider each item in your pack, and you realize that you have nothing to help the Sherpas.

You shrug and say, "Good luck."

Nawa bows, and then the Sherpas disappear into the raging storm.

Turn to page 73.

"Can't stop," you tell him. "Not in . . . this weather."

The blue climber nods, and you struggle back to your feet. It is difficult to do. You are drained of energy, both physically and mentally. Snow swirls all around you. You want nothing more than to lie down, curl into a ball and rest. But you know that if you stay too long, you might never get up.

You pull Zoey out of the snow, and the blue climber helps you gather the others. When everyone is up and moving, you once again lead them downward. It is nearly impossible to see where you're going, but this is a much wiser option than waiting to freeze to death.

The going is slow. You aren't sure where you are, and you know that each step could be your last. You move cautiously, trying to remember to test the snow before putting your full weight on it. But your mind is as hazy as the weather. Your body teeters with every movement. You can barely catch your breath. It takes everything in you just to keep going.

You take another step, and your foot meets nothing. You tumble forward, and suddenly you are sliding. You feel a short tug on your rope, but it quickly gives.

Zoey has fallen too.

Too late, you realize your mistake. You should have guessed where on the mountain you are. You've been blindly traversing the Knife Ridge—it was only a matter of time before you veered the wrong way. Your error in judgment will cost your life, your sister's and perhaps the others who are with you.

Now, you can only flail wildly, unable to find footing. Your hands grasp a rocky ledge just as your body slips over it. You are left hanging at the edge of a cliff.

The muscles in your arms burn like fire. You feel them cracking and tearing as you struggle to hold on. But all too soon, the pain becomes too much to bear. You cannot hold on any longer, so you do the only thing you can.

You let go.

For a moment, you are falling. The mountain zips past your eyes, and you hear the beginning of a scream. But that noise is cut off by a loud *thunk*. It is the last sound you ever hear.

Turn to page 67.

The only thing more dangerous than venturing down the mountain is waiting in this cold. You cannot just sit here and watch your sister die. You pull Zoey to her feet. That alone takes several long minutes. She doesn't have the strength to stand, so you must do the work for her.

You drape her arm over your shoulders and hold it in place with your hand. You wrap your other hand around her waist and pull her close to you.

"Okay, Zo," you tell her. "We'll take it nice and easy. Just step when I step."

Zoey nods, and you begin on your way.

Progress is slow. Your body aches, switching between the burning sensation of tired muscles and a coldness unlike any other. You're not sure where you are, and Zoey is weighing you down. She can't walk on her own, and she can barely walk with you helping her. In fact, it feels as if you are mostly just dragging her down the mountain.

You are almost as exhausted as she is, and it makes you careless. You focus on your pain. You stop paying attention to anything else, like the mountain beneath you.

The snow below your left foot gives, and you slip. You let go of your sister and tumble into the snow. Suddenly you're sliding. You flail wildly, unable to find any footing. Your hands grasp a rocky ledge just as your body slips over it. You are left hanging at the edge of a cliff.

The muscles in your arms burn like fire. You feel them cracking and tearing as you struggle to hold on. But all too soon, the pain becomes too much to bear. You cannot hold on any longer, so you do the only thing you can.

You let go.

For a moment, you are falling. The mountain zips past your eyes, and you hear the beginning of a scream. But that noise is cut off by a loud *thunk*. It is the last sound you ever hear.

Turn to page 67.

You don't have extra gloves, but Zoey brought extra glove liners. They're better than nothing. You pull them out of her backpack and, as carefully as you can, slide Zoey's hands into them. She doesn't say anything, but she doesn't fight you either. At this point, you'll take it. Sadly, at best, she'll probably lose a few of her fingers.

You help your sister to her feet, which isn't easy given that your head is spinning and you can barely stand, yourself. Gusts of wind threaten to push you over. You wish you could sit back down and stay there.

The other climbers, even the one with the blue jacket, remain huddled in a tight group.

"It's lighter out. Let's go," you say between gasps.

No one responds.

The blue climber looks up and shakes his head. He mumbles something you can't hear. It seems that, in the time since he punched you, your roles have reversed.

Precious seconds tick by. You need to get moving. Who can guess when the storm will kick back up? You have to take advantage of this break in the weather. But you also know if the others stay, they will likely die. The blue climber saved your life. Should you try to do the same for him? What will you choose to do?

If you and Zoey leave now, you may reach Camp Four before the storm revs up again. But the others will probably die if they don't come with you. They're close to gone already, and this is their only shot at survival.

If you stay until you can convince the others to come, you may end up saving their lives. But each shred of energy you spend trying to bring them with you is energy you won't have to get yourself and Zoey back to safety.

If you choose to leave now, turn to page 83.

If you choose to help the others, turn to page 87.

Even if you could find Zoey on your own, you don't have the strength to rescue her—not by yourself. You hurry out of your tent and back into the blinding storm. Snow whips and whirls around you. The wind claws and scratches at your protective clothing. You can barely make out the shape of the tent nearest yours. But you see it, and you rush to it.

You check inside, shouting, "Ned!" The tent is empty.

You check the next tent and the next. "Ned, where are you?" you cry, again and again.

Many of the tents are vacant. The occupied ones offer moments of hope, but your uncle is nowhere to be found. And while most of the climbers are too weak to talk, the ones who answer cannot guess where Ned might be.

Minutes tick away. Time is running out on your sister. By now, even if you wanted to change your mind—to go up the mountain alone—you know it's too late. A rescue team is Zoey's only chance.

You wander through the camp, checking your own tent once more. Leslie is asleep, but no one is with her. You circle through each tent a second time. The results are the same.

You return to the central tent. It is your last hope.

The moment you step inside, Nawa grabs you. "There you are. Ned try to find you."

Your eyes widen. "Uncle Ned? Where is he?"

"He looking for you. He walking around camp."

Is it possible? Have the two of you been searching this same, small area for each other? How could you have missed him? The wind howls outside, as if to answer your question; you can't see more than a few feet in front of your face out there.

You grab Nawa's shoulders. "Okay, listen. This is very important. I'm going back to my tent. I'll wait for Ned there. Tell him to meet me in my tent."

Nawa nods. "I tell him."

"Thank you, Nawa. And please tell him to hurry."

You sit and wait. The tent's nylon walls ripple in the wind. The endless flapping of fabric makes a deafening noise. You're forced to sit with your back to the wind, leaning against one of the tent poles, just to ensure that your shelter doesn't rip in two.

You're not sure how long you've been waiting, but it seems like an eternity. You're stuck, worrying about your sister and watching Leslie sleep. Right now, you can do nothing for either of them. You've never felt so helpless in your life.

The front of your tent shakes, and the zipper slides open. Uncle Ned stumbles inside. The gear that covers him is peppered with chunks of ice and snow.

"Zach, thank God!" your uncle exclaims. He quickly hugs you.

"We have to help Zo," you blurt. "She's still up there."

Your uncle listens while you explain your story. If the news rattles him, he does not show it. He remains calm and attentive, although perhaps the day's tragedies have numbed him to the emotions of panic and fear.

You finish your narrative, and Ned simply nods. He pats your leg and climbs to his knees.

"Wait here," he tells you. "I'll find her."

He turns to leave, but you grab his arm. "She's my sister. I'm coming too."

"No, Zach," he answers.

"But I know where she is. I'll lead you to her."

Ned shakes his head. "You told me where she is, and we both know she doesn't have much time. If you come, you'll just slow me down."

You let go of your uncle and slump into your spot.

You know he's right, but it doesn't make you feel any better to hear it.

"Besides," he adds, trying to sound upbeat. "Leslie is here. She looks like she's going to make it, thanks to you. Your job is to keep her alive."

With that, Uncle Ned turns and zips out of the tent, disappearing into the blizzard.

Turn to page 92.

It's a difficult decision, but you know what you must do. Zoey is in your care. Her life depends on you. You'll need all of your strength to get her down the mountain. That means you don't have any oxygen to spare.

You lift your sister off the frozen surface. It feels like you're trying to carry a car. You're already weakened, and your gear only makes matters worse. You drop Zoey in favor of a new decision. The only way you'll get her to Camp Four is if you rid yourself of the extra weight you're carrying. You dump the largest, bulkiest items out of your backpack in favor of your sister, and you pull her off the ground again.

She is almost completely out of it. She offers no help at all as you move downward. You're left yanking her along the ground, one step at a time.

Turn to the next page.

Your back quickly begins to ache, and you're surprised to see that you've only moved about 20 feet. You need a different approach.

You pull Zoey up again, this time hoisting her over your shoulder. It works better, allowing you to move more quickly. But her weight throws off your balance. You stumble and teeter slowly downward, concentrating hard not to fall.

You are making progress, but one false move—one misstep—could be the end of you both. Plus, you're not sure how much longer you can hold her. You consider your decision to keep your oxygen and wonder if you should change your mind. Is is better to stick with your original plan, or should you try Plan B? What will you choose to do?

If you choose to keep your plan, turn to page 126.

If you choose to change your mind, turn to page 90.

7

KNIFE RIDGE

You inch your way down the mountain. The storm rages around you, tearing at you and your sister with shrieking claws of wind and snow. Bits of ice slice at your face. You wonder if the next step will be your last.

You stop, and Zoey stumbles into you.

"We should . . . tie together," you shout. The wind crushes your words as they leave your mouth.

Zoey just stands in place, bent against the storm.

You grab an extra short rope from your pack, aware that every second you're stopped is a second closer to death. You shake as you loop a rope between your harness and Zoey's. She doesn't seem to know what you're doing.

You give the rope a tug and hope the knots will hold. You start inching forward again, silently praying that you won't walk off a cliff.

The rope suddenly yanks you backward. Your arms pinwheel as you fight to stay on your feet. You look back at Zoey. She stands motionless.

You regain your balance and tug on the rope. Zoey moves one shuffling step toward you. You can barely see her. Then an obvious idea hits you—one you should have considered hours ago. You switch on your headlamp.

In a way, it makes seeing even harder. The snow whips past the light fast and furiously; it looks as if you are walking into a TV screen of static. But it makes you feel better. And at least you can see Zoey now.

You haul your sister down the mountain, one tug at a time. Your strength is failing fast, and so is your mind. Shadowy forms prowl at the corners of your vision. Is that a lion? Or a pack of wolves? They can't be real, can they?

You turn and take a few steps backward, checking on Zoey. But then you bump into something completely unexpected: another climber.

It's impossible to tell who it is. The heavy, blue jacket looks like everyone else's in this stormy weather. The cap, mask, goggles and hood make it impossible to see any facial features. You think it's a man, but you can't even be sure of that.

You spot three more climbers huddled nearby. The blue climber is in better condition than the others. The rest of them look worse off than Zoey. One of them isn't wearing a mask; his (or her) face is covered in purple and black patches.

"Is this . . . the trail? Are you on . . . it?" you ask the blue climber, shouting over the wind.

The blue climber shakes his head. "Lost it!"

"Us, too. This way . . . I think. Go . . . together?"

The wind roars loudly as the blue climber answers. You don't understand him. He nods though, and you take that to mean he agrees.

"Can the . . . others . . . make it?" you ask.

His lack of response reveals that he can no longer hear you either. You point to his group of three. He nods again, and then he slowly gets the others up and moving.

Your new team edges forward. You can't see anything until you're right on top of it. You must test each step before putting your weight down. You weave through giant outcroppings of shale. You repeatedly swing your ice axe into the snow beside your boots.

The axe suddenly swings into nothing.

Whoosh!

A giant crevasse opens. You stumble back from the edge just in time, your stomach doing flips inside you.

You swing your head around, shouting a warning to the others. Thankfully, they hear you and stop.

You walk your way along the rope tied to Zoey until you reach her. You lead her away from the crevasse. When your backs hit rock, you slide down in exhaustion.

Your headlamp guides the other four climbers to you, safely away from the deadly crevasse. One by one they collapse beside you and Zoey.

If it's even possible, the weather seems worse. The wind howls with new intensity. Even sitting down, it's hard to stay in place without the wind bowling you over. The darkness is complete. Without the headlamp, you doubt you could even see your hand in front of your face.

"Should we keep going?" the blue climber yells. "Or do we wait out the storm?"

What will you choose to do?

The faster you get to Camp Four, the better your chances of making it through this alive. If you stay where you are, you run the very real risk of freezing to death.

However, you're stumbling blindly down a mountain. That's a dangerous decision in any conditions. You can't see where you're going, and one misstep could be the end of you.

If you wait, the weather may clear soon, making it easier to see where you're going.

If you choose to keep going, turn to page 96.

If you choose to stay and wait, turn to page 76.

You know you're right. You trust your instincts. The compass must be broken. You veer away from the left path, trudging upward through the deadly storm.

The going becomes more difficult with every step. Even with your mask providing oxygen, you find it hard to breathe. Your brain commands your legs to move, but they are too tired to cooperate. Only the thought of your dying sister propels you onward, but you must rest for at least seven or eight breaths between each movement.

You are climbing too slowly, and you know it. But there is nothing else you can do. You are exhausted.

You daydream about your tent and your sleeping bag. You should be inside both of them right now, resting and recovering. Zoey fades from your memory. Instead, you concentrate on your weary muscles and the bitter cold that bites you.

How long have you been climbing? You cannot be certain, but it's been too long; you should have found your sister by now.

A voice inside you shouts, "You went the wrong way!" This thought is paralyzing. You know that you shouldn't, but you cannot help yourself: You plop into the snow and ice beneath your feet.

You are trapped between two ideas. Are you moving in the wrong direction? If so, you're getting farther from your sister. Or are you on the right path? In that case, you might find her any minute.

Your mind is torn. You cannot decide what to do, which way to go. So you do nothing. You remain there, lost and alone.

Eventually, your inner voice calms. The cold's sharp, stabbing pain becomes numbness. Your eyes grow heavy, so you close them. You imagine yourself standing up, pressing onward and finding your sister—alive and well. You are overwhelmed with joy. You hug her as tears stream down your face.

You believe that your mission is at an end, yet it is all happening inside your mind. And before long, even that dream fades. You slip into a deep sleep—a sleep from which you will never awaken.

Turn to page 67.

You pull the extra gloves out of your backpack and, as carefully as you can, slide Zoey's hands into them. She doesn't say anything, but she doesn't fight you either. At this point, you'll take it. You only hope it's not too late to save her fingers.

You help your sister to her feet, which isn't easy given that your head is spinning and you can barely stand. Gusts of wind threaten to push you over. You wish you could sit back down and stay there.

The other climbers, even the one with the blue jacket, remain huddled in a tight group.

"It's lighter out. Let's go," you say between gasps.

No one responds.

"Come on!"

The blue climber looks up and shakes his head. He mumbles something you can't hear. It seems that, in the time since he punched you, your roles have reversed.

Precious seconds tick by. You need to get moving. Who can guess when the storm will kick back up? You have to take advantage of this break in the weather. But you also know if the others stay, they will likely die. The blue climber saved your life. Should you try to do the same for him? What will you choose to do?

If you and Zoey leave now, you may reach Camp Four before the storm revs up again. But the others will probably die if they don't come with you. They're close to gone already, and this is their only shot at survival.

If you stay until you can convince the others to come, you may end up saving their lives. But each shred of energy you spend trying to bring them with you is energy you won't have to get yourself and Zoey back to safety.

If you choose to leave now, turn to page 83.

If you choose to help the others, turn to page 87.

You quickly tug the pack off your back and dig inside. "Here," you say to Nawa, "take this. You can add it to your end of the rope. It'll give you more room to wander away from us."

Nawa bows in gratitude and ties your rope to his. Then the Sherpas disappear into the storm.

Turn to page 73.

9

UPS AND DOWNS

Your eyes open slowly. You don't know if you've been asleep for two minutes or two hours. The yellow walls of your tent shake and snap, but at least they keep out the deadly wind.

You turn and check on your sister. She lies motionless on her sleeping bag, still wearing her gear. It's hard to tell with everything on, but you see a slight rise and fall. That means she's breathing.

The last thing you want to do is open the front of your tent and step back into the storm—but that's exactly what happens. You're hoping to find Uncle Ned or one of the Sherpas from your team, anyone who can help Zoey. But Camp Four is in chaos. The break in the storm is over; the blizzard is back and worse than ever.

Some of the tents have collapsed and whip wildly in the wind. As you watch the tents, a climber stumbles past. You grab his arm.

"Have you seen Ned Manning?" you shout.

The person shakes you off and staggers from tent to tent, probably looking for someone, too. You see others doing the same thing. You may never find Uncle Ned in this confusing mess.

A sudden gust pushes you to your knees. You look up to find your team's stockpile of oxygen canisters. You paw through them and find two extras. Then, with a canister under each arm, you rush back to your tent.

You quickly hook up the fresh canisters, first Zoey's, then yours. The fresh flow of oxygen tastes like life itself. Within a few breaths, you feel sharper and stronger. Zoey moans quietly behind her mask. Any noise is better than no noise.

You prepare a hot thermos of tea. That and the fresh oxygen should help your sister. You concentrate hard just to hold the thermos. Your hands shake so much that some of the tea splashes onto your sleeping bag. You carefully crawl to your sister.

"C'mon, Zo," you say. "Let's get you out of your gear and into your bag. I've got some hot tea for you." Your voice shakes as much as your hands.

You fumble with the drawstring on Zoey's hood and then pull the hood back from her face.

You blink in confusion. A terrible realization dawns on you. Zoey's cap should be purple, but it's green instead. Her hair looks red, not blonde.

"Oh, no," you whisper. "No, no, no, no!"

With quaking hands, you remove the oxygen mask, praying that you'll see your sister staring back at you.

Instead, it is Leslie Quaid who moans and opens her eyes. "Where am I?" she slurs.

You swallow hard. Tears sting your eyes. Up there, in the storm, you grabbed the wrong person. Zoey is still on the mountain.

You fight the rising panic. You get Leslie to sit up, and you shove the hot tea into her hands. "Drink this," you tell her. Then you barrel back into the storm, desperate to find your uncle.

If anything, Camp Four looks worse than before. Headlamps, muffled by frenzied swirls of snow, pepper the camp in eerie, bobbing paths. The wind grabs your body and shoves you back and forth. You stumble toward Uncle Ned's tent—at least you hope it's his tent.

A larger, blue bubble looms out of the darkness. It's one of the central tents, big enough for several climbers to fit inside.

You burst inside. Injured climbers are stretched out on the tables, while other climbers tend to them. You duck as one of the "doctors" throws a sterile package of bandages across the tent to another. Battery-powered lanterns swing from the top poles.

A climber, entering the tent behind you, bumps you aside. Another trips you, and you end up on your knees. A strong arm pulls you to your feet. You look up and see a smiling Sherpa with a red cap.

"Nawa!" you exclaim.

The Sherpa tugs you into a quick hug. "You okay!"

"Where is everyone?" you ask.

Nawa shakes his head sadly. "Many missing. Others not so—"

"What about Ned?" you interrupt.

"He okay," says Nawa. "Here just minute past."

"He was here? Where did he go?"

Nawa points toward the tent opening. "Out. Said find you and Zoey."

"Thanks, Nawa," you shout, as you rush back outside.

You retrace your steps. If Uncle Ned is looking for you and Zoey, your best bet of finding him is probably back at your tent.

But when you stagger inside, only Leslie Quaid is there. It looks like she's had some of the tea, but she forgot to put her oxygen mask back on.

"When is the plane coming?" she asks. She's obviously pretty out of it: There will be no planes landing this high up, on a mountain, in the middle of a storm.

You help her slip her mask back into place. "Soon," you lie. "Real soon."

Leslie nods and settles back into her sleeping bag—Zoey's sleeping bag. Your throat tightens. While Leslie cozies up in her sleeping bag, Zoey is fighting for her life up the mountain.

You can't just leave her there, so you have a choice to make. You can either try to find Uncle Ned and mount a team rescue, or you can go right now and try to rescue Zoey yourself. What will you choose to do?

A search for Uncle Ned will take time, wasting precious minutes that your sister may not have. If you leave now, you'll likely reach her more quickly, and speed in these conditions means survival.

However, your uncle Ned has more experience. He can quickly organize a team to assist with the rescue effort. He will be better able to reach your sister and to help her when he does. The question is, will you be able to find him in time?

If you choose to search for Ned, turn to page 102.

If you choose to leave now, turn to page 94.

In a survival situation, one of the most dangerous things you can do is second-guess your decisions. You have made your choice, and you're sticking with it. You continue trudging downward, through the blinding storm, breathing in the oxygen that provides what little strength remains.

Your footing is unsure. You try to aim your footfalls, but you miss the mark every time. It becomes something of a game—anything to keep your mind off your muscles' burning pain and the frigid cold that threatens to take you and your sister.

You miss. You miss again. The next time you hit your spot, but only because you slipped.

Suddenly, the wind roars to a deafening crescendo, and your game comes to an end. You can no longer see your feet.

You step once more, and the snow beneath your left foot gives. You slip, losing hold of your sister. You tumble into the snow, and suddenly you're sliding.

You flail wildly, unable to find any footing. Your hands grasp a rocky ledge just as your body slips over it. You are left hanging at the edge of a cliff.

The muscles in your arms burn like fire. You feel them cracking and tearing as you struggle to hold on. But all too soon, the pain becomes too much to bear. You cannot hold on any longer, so you do the only thing you can.

You let go.

For a moment, you are falling. The mountain zips past your eyes, and you hear the beginning of a scream. But that noise is cut off by a loud *thunk*. It is the last sound you ever hear.

Turn to page 67.

You unhook your canister and take off your mask. Your first breath of Everest's thin air feels like a thousand knives stabbing your lungs. You collapse into the snow, gasping, feeling as if you're drowning.

You don't know how long you stay there. But slowly you adjust, inhaling five quick breaths between each small movement. You crawl to Zoey and hook your oxygen canister to her mask. Then you cross your fingers, and you wait.

Zoey gasps and her eyes open. "Zach?"

You grab your twin sister in a bear hug. "I . . . thought I'd . . . lost you."

"I remember Nawa and Jigmi going that way," she replies, pointing weakly. But then she bites her lip. "Or that way." She points in the opposite direction.

"We have to . . . keep going. I don't . . . think . . . they're coming back." Your words are stilted, cut off by short, gasping breaths.

Zoey lurches to a stand and grabs her pack. She helps you with your own. You feel a twinge of guilt, but you leave the empty oxygen canisters behind. The less weight the better.

Your sister takes off her mask and hands it to you. She sways on her feet. You take a couple of breaths, then hand her mask back.

You and Zoey pick the direction that you think the Sherpas took. You start down the mountain, into the heart of the storm.

Turn to page 108.

You quickly tug the pack off your back and dig inside. "Here," you say to Nawa, "take this."

You hand him your GPS, and then you blush. His look asks the question you're asking yourself. *Why didn't we use this sooner?*

You shrug, blaming it on the thin air affecting your ability to think clearly.

"Take it and go," you say to Nawa.

He bows in gratitude, and then the Sherpas disappear into the storm.

Turn to page 73.

11

STRANGE LIGHT

It feels like you've been here forever, like you've never known anything else. In the darkness, you start to feel detached. It's like you're watching yourself from a great distance. The pain in your hands and feet gradually fades away. An odd sense of warmth wraps around you. You become aware that you are slowly dying.

A strange, glowing light appears. Is this it? Is this the light at the end of the tunnel? Has the end arrived for you? A brief panic pierces your calm. You don't want to die; you want to live—if only to save your sister.

The light grows stronger, closer. It explodes over the mountain peaks. You were wrong. This isn't the end. It's the beginning. You've made it through the night. You're watching the sunrise!

A spark of hope ignites deep within your frozen mind. You cannot move; you can't even turn to see if Zoey is all right. But you cling to that hope. Your body has shut down just about every system. All you can do now is wait.

You fade in and out. Sometimes the white rabbit comes and sits beside you. You don't mind.

You hear a crunch, and the white rabbit disappears in a sparkling explosion of snow. You hear another crunch, then another.

Like a dream, a climber in a bright red jacket appears in front of you. You'd blink in surprise if your eyelids weren't frozen. Four more climbers fan out to the rest of your huddled group. They hook up new oxygen canisters to everyone's masks.

With your first breath of fresh oxygen, you know it's not a dream. The rescue team you hoped for is here.

The oxygen gives you a brief boost, and you're able to turn toward your sister. She's being helped, too. Zoey's still alive.

Slowly, slowly, they help you to your feet and get you moving down the mountain. What felt like days last night takes mere minutes in the sunlight. In no time at all, you're stretched out on a table inside a big blue tent at one of the camps—you're not sure which.

A camp doctor checks you over. You feel okay, just completely wiped out. You hear a commotion at the front of the tent. Then Uncle Ned rushes to your side.

He grabs you in a huge hug, almost pulling you off the table. "Zach! You're okay!" He plunks you back onto the table and asks the doctor, "Is he okay?"

The doctor smiles. "Aside from dehydration and some minor frostbite, I'd say he's all right. You've got one lucky nephew, Ned."

"What about Zoey?" you ask.

Ned pats your shoulder. "She's going to be . . . fine."

"What do you mean *fine*?" you ask.

Ned looks at the doctor. "It's okay," says the doc. "You can tell him."

Your uncle takes a deep breath. "Your sister took a real beating on that mountain. She'll probably lose a couple of toes . . . and maybe a finger or two."

You swallow hard. "Poor Zoey."

From the next table over you hear, "I'm not poor anything! Do you realize you'll be doing the dishes alone for, like, ever?"

You ignore the doctor's protests and launch yourself from your table. You tackle your sister in a bear hug.

"Ow!" she yelps. "Careful, my hands!"

"Sorry, Zo." You step back, and Zoey holds up her bandaged hands. Her feet are bandaged, too.

She takes your hand gently in her bandaged ones. "Thank you for saving my life, Zach. I wouldn't have made it if you didn't come back for me."

You're not sure what to say. You accomplished what you set out to do, but reaching your goal came at a price. You almost lost your twin sister.

Zoey gives you a nudge. "Hey, we did it. I am now the youngest climber ever to summit Mount Everest."

"You? What about me?"

Zoey grins. "Too bad. You were born three minutes before me. That makes me the youngest."

Together, you are helped back to Base Camp. It is a dangerous trip, but you are aided by the best of climbers. You are loaded onto a helicopter, which takes you farther into Nepal where your parents, and nearly 100 reporters, are waiting for you.

You have a new respect for Mount Everest and for the power of nature. You look at your sister and smile. You can't help but think that the mountain almost beat you. But it also taught you what's really important: each other.

Turn to the next page.

CONGRATULATIONS!

YOU SURVIVED THE STORM AT THE SUMMIT OF MOUNT EVEREST

IF YOU LIKED THIS STORY,
YOU MIGHT ALSO ENJOY ...

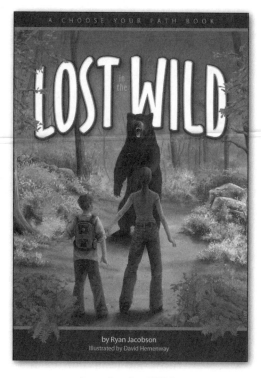

**Lost in the Wild:
A Choose Your Path Book**

THE EFFECTS OF HIGH ALTITUDE

Our bodies react to changes in altitude, especially if those changes are extreme. Have you ever taken a car trip and felt your ears plug as you went down a big hill? Or maybe you've been on a plane and felt your ears pop. That's because the air is thinner the higher you go. The air in your ears is pressing harder against your eardrums than the air outside your ears. Your body must equalize the pressure, and this is what causes the pop.

When air pressure around you is less than what you're used to, your body scrambles to adjust. Your heart will beat faster to move more blood. You'll breathe quickly to pull in more oxygen. You'll even go to the bathroom more often—everything is working faster. You'll also need to drink more water, and it's hard to sleep. Worst of all, you can get dangerously sick.

Acute Mountain Sickness (AMS) can affect people who are climbing, hiking, skiing or traveling above 8,000 feet. For that matter, an altitude from 5,000 to 11,500 feet above sea level is considered high. Very high altitude is between 11,500 and 18,000 feet. Anything greater than 18,000 feet, like Zoey and Zach's climb, is called extreme altitude. That's three and a half miles up!

AMS is caused by reduced air pressure and less oxygen for your body to use. Most people who climb above 10,000 feet will feel at least some of these mild symptoms:

- dizziness
- extreme tiredness
- headache and/or stomach ache
- difficult breathing
- racing heart

If a climber with these symptoms keeps going, he or she risks developing severe AMS:

- bluish skin
- confused thinking
- blackouts
- difficulty moving
- strange behavior

If the AMS is mild, symptoms might lessen with rest or as climbers get used to new altitudes. If the AMS is severe, sick climbers must be quickly brought down to lower altitudes, or they could eventually die.

You may notice that Zach and Zoey got away with a few wrong choices—because they're book characters!

EVEREST'S YOUNGEST CLIMBER

The youngest person to reach Mount Everest's summit is American climber Jordan Romero. On May 22, 2010, Jordan stepped into history at 13 years, 10 months, 10 days old. He lives in California and climbs with his dad, Paul Romero, and his stepmom, Karen Lundgren. On his historic Everest climb, Jordan's team also included three Sherpas: Ang Pasang Sherpa, Lama Dawa Sherpa and Lama Kharma Sherpa.

Climbing Mount Everest was part of Jordan's bigger goal: to become the youngest person to climb the Seven Summits, the highest mountains on each continent. He set that goal when he was only nine years old. He saw a painting in the hallway of his school showing the peaks and dared to dream big.

When he's not training or climbing, Jordan shares his experiences with other kids, families and communities. He stresses goal-setting, working as part of a team with your family, eating healthy and being active outdoors.

"I did it, so can you. Find your Everest."
—Jordan Romero

OTHER FAMOUS CLIMBERS

Sir Edmund Hillary and **Tenzing Norgay** were the first people ever to reach the summit of Mount Everest. They accomplished this feat on May 29, 1953. Hillary was a climber from New Zealand. Tenzing Norgay was a Nepalese Sherpa.

George Mallory was a British climber who led three attempts to summit Mount Everest in the 1920s. In 1924, he and his climbing partner, **Andrew Irvine**, died on the mountain. Some people believe they were the first ever to reach the summit, but this has never been proven.

Reinhold Messner and **Peter Habeler** made history in 1978, when they became the first climbers to summit Mount Everest without oxygen tanks or supplemental oxygen. Messner was a climber from Italy. Habeler was from Austria.

Jon Krakauer, a U.S. climber, gained fame from his book, *Into Thin Air*. The novel tells his story about a 1996 Everest expedition. On the way down, he and many other climbers were caught in a deadly storm.

ABOUT RYAN JACOBSON

Photograph by Cheryl Rozek

Ryan Jacobson has never climbed a mountain. The closest he's ever come was playing King of the Hill in his youth. But he has always been fascinated by mountain climbers and with Mount Everest in particular. He got the idea for writing *Storm at the Summit of Mount Everest* from his wife, Lora.

Ryan is the author of nearly 20 books, including picture books, graphic novels, chapter books, ghost stories and choose your path books.

Ryan lives in Mora, Minnesota, with his wife Lora, sons Jonah and Lucas, and dog Boo. For more about Ryan, visit www.RyanJacobsonOnline.com.

ABOUT DEB MERCIER

Deb Mercier loves the outdoors. You can often find her walking her dog—though not on any mountain slopes to date. The toughest hike she's ever done was to the top of Angel's Landing in Zion National Park. She doesn't dare go any higher, mostly because she's scared of heights! Her writing credits include several middle-grade books, two picture books and a long-running newspaper column.

Deb and her family live in rural Minnesota. She volunteers at Minnewaska Area Schools, loves good pizza and saves turtles from roadways whenever possible. For more information about Deb and her latest projects, visit www.debmercier.com.

SELECTED BIBLIOGRAPHY

Alan Arnette. www.alanarnette.com. Alan Arnette, 2011.

Bio: True Story. www.biography.com. A&E Television Networks, 2011.

ExplorersWeb. www.explorersweb.com. ExplorersWeb, Inc., 2011.

How Stuff Works. http://adventure.howstuffworks.com. HowStuffWorks, Inc., 2011.

Into Thin Air: A Personal Account of the Mount Everest Disaster. Jon Krakauer. Random House, New York, 1997.

Jordan Romero. www.jordanromero.com. Jordan Romero, 2011.

PBS Online. www.pbs.org. Public Broadcasting Service, 2011.

Frontline: Storm Over Everest. David Breashears. Public Broadcasting Service, Arlington, VA. 2008.

U.S. National Library of Medicine. www.nlm.nih.gov.

Wildest Dream: The Biography of George Mallory. Peter and Leni Gillman. Mountaineers Books, Seattle. 2000.